Lighthouse Lock Out

EGMONT

We bring stories to life

First published in Great Britain in 2013
by Egmont UK Limited, The Yellow Building,
1 Nicholas Road, London W11 4AN

HiT entertainment

ISBN 978 1 4052 6981 0
56313/2

KU-204-097

Fireman Sam, Penny and Elvis were practising rescue drills in the forest.

"That's enough for one day," said Fireman Sam, jumping into Jupiter and revving the engine.

Jupiter's wheels span around
and around, but it didn't move.
"**Oh no,**" cried Sam. "**We're
stuck in the mud!**"

Back in Pontypandy, Norman and Mandy were having a mud fight. Mike's van got covered in mud!

"You're not going anywhere until you have washed that van," said Helen.

"But Mike is giving us a tour of the lighthouse," said Norman. "We'll wash it when we get back."

In the forest, Fireman Sam used Venus to pull Jupiter out of the mud. Both trucks were covered in dirt!

"I'm not looking forward to washing those two!" chuckled Elvis.

Meanwhile, Norman, Mandy, Helen and Dilys were enjoying Mike's lighthouse tour.

"I'll wedge the door open so it can't swing shut," said Mike.

"We can't stay too long," said Dilys.

"We've got to get back to wash Mike's van," Helen whispered to the children.

"I know how to get out of washing that van," muttered Norman.

He stretched out his leg and kicked the wedge away from the door.

CLUNK! The heavy door slammed shut.

"**Oopsie**," said Norman.

"**Oooo, Norman**," gasped Mandy.

"**Norman!** You naughty boy,"
cried Dilys, trying the handle.
"Now the door is locked!"

"Let's phone for help," said
Helen.

"Erm ... my phone is in the van,"
gulped Mike.

"Don't worry," said Mandy.
"I can see Moose down below.
Over here, Moose!"

Moose raced up to the lighthouse to help his friends.

"What the grizzlies is going on here?" he asked.

"We got locked out!" explained Helen.

"I'm **not** going to wash that van," muttered Norman. "**Hey, everyone,** look at that giant bird."

When everyone turned to look, Norman kicked the door shut **again!**

"Norman! Not again!" gasped Mike. "How are we going to get down now?"

"Moose, what's that?" Mandy asked, pointing to a rope in Moose's backpack. "Can you use that to get down?"

"No problem," smiled Moose. He tied the rope to the railings and began to abseil down the lighthouse.

"**Are you at the bottom yet?**"
Mike shouted down
the lighthouse.

"Not quite," replied Moose.
"The rope isn't long enough.
I'm stuck!"

"We need Fireman Sam!" said
Mandy. "Moose, can you
send a flare into the sky?"

Moose pulled a flare out of
his backpack. "Stand back
everyone. Here goes!"

The flare lit up the sky.
Fireman Sam saw it
right away.

When he found Moose
dangling from the
lighthouse, he called
for back-up.

"Tom, we need your
helicopter – and fast!"

When the helicopter arrived, Tom lifted Fireman Sam high into the air.

Fireman Sam attached Moose to the harness and Tom lowered them both to safety.

"**Phew!** That was a close call!" said Moose.

Later that day, Norman and Mandy were finally washing Mike's van when Fireman Sam pulled up.

"I've heard how much you love washing, Norman, so I've brought some more work for you," smiled Sam, pointing at Jupiter and Venus.

"**Oh no!**" groaned Norman.